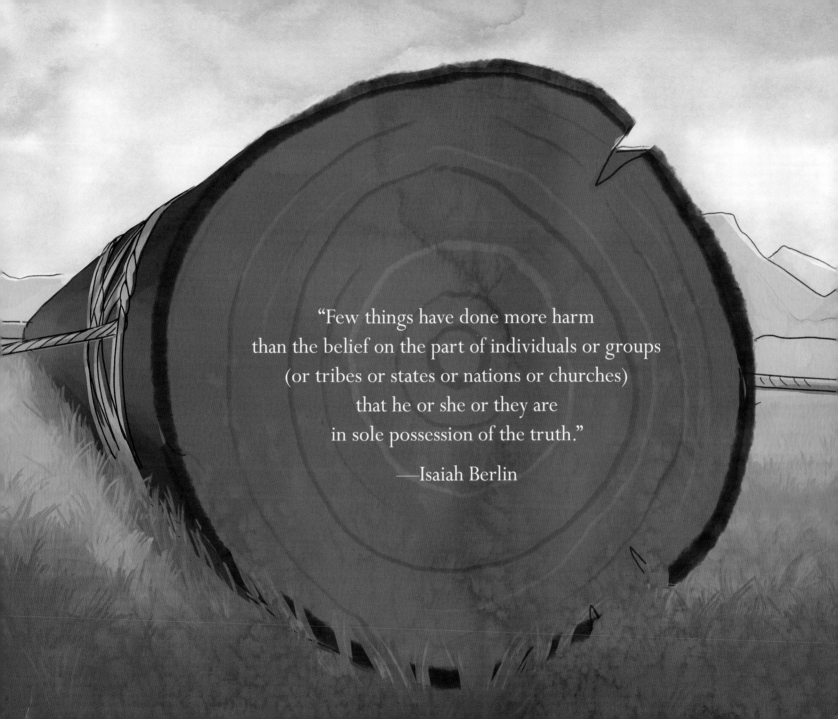

"Few things have done more harm
than the belief on the part of individuals or groups
(or tribes or states or nations or churches)
that he or she or they are
in sole possession of the truth."

—Isaiah Berlin

If you're reading this, then Tyler Storlie is now, to his great surprise, a children's book author. Prior to writing *Two Tribes*, Tyler worked in healthcare IT, managed operations for the family business, and built schools in Nepal as a volunteer. Tyler has a degree in mechanical engineering from Washington University in St. Louis and currently lives in his hometown of Minneapolis, Minnesota.

ISBN 13: 978-1-63489-239-1

Printed in the United States of America

First Printing: 2019

23 22 21 20 19   5 4 3 2 1

Cover and interior design by Dan Pitts.

807 Broadway St. NE, Suite 46
Minneapolis, MN 55413
wiseink.com

Written by TYLER STORLIE • Illustrated by RACHEL BEENKEN

TWO TRIBES

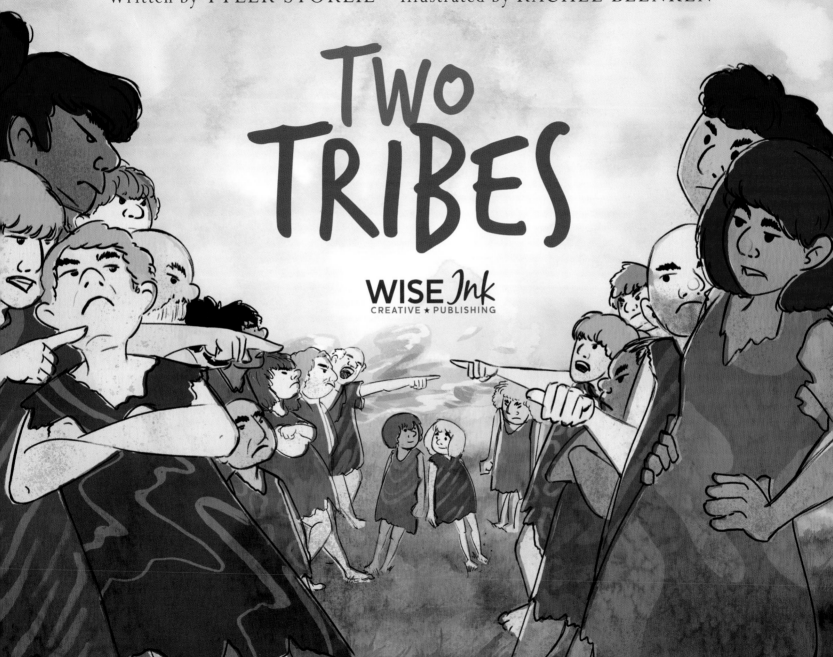

In a land nearby but a time long ago,
Two different tribes shared a village called Home.

In a beautiful valley between mountains and streams,
The two tribes found a giant old tree.

It was under the tree where they first took shelter,
So they called the tree sacred and lived around it together.

But there was something peculiar about these two tribes
That caused them to drift apart over time.

One tribe had left legs longer than right,
And the other had right legs longer than left.

Now, don't be concerned, there's nothing to fret.
Their leans were quite natural, and let's not forget

That right-leaners and left-leaners aren't as different as they seem.
They all want what's best for their Home under the tree.

But the two tribes were stubborn and filled with pride,
For each believed they were the better side.

And with their strong leans, neither could see
Why the other tribe walked so differently.

As you might imagine, they argued when they talked,
And avoided each other on the paths where they walked.

So although they all shared this village called Home,
They stuck with their own tribes
And chose not to roam.

"It's totally crooked!"

"Looks good to me!"

Then one day, something terrible happened—

High in the mountains overlooking the tree,
A dam was broken. The water broke free.

The river ran fast. The water spilled out
Into the valley, toward the village it spout.

The flood spread quickly over the land,
And the two tribes were forced to come up with a plan.

Without time to think and feeling quite rushed,
They started to panic and weren't sure who to trust.

They bickered and argued about what to do,
Until a wise elder spoke the unspeakable truth.

"We have to cut down the old sacred tree.
It's the only thing big enough to plug the dam's giant leak!"

The two tribes were sad, but they knew it was true,
So they chopped down the tree with an ax swing or two.

The left-leaners on the left, the right-leaners on the right,
Tied two ropes around it and pulled with all their might.

But the right-leaners leaned right and the left-leaners leaned left,
And away from the middle they moved as they went.

But nobody noticed, because nobody talked,
And they struggled in silence as they pulled and they walked.

Not until pulling got harder and harder
Did they stop to ask why they hadn't gone farther.

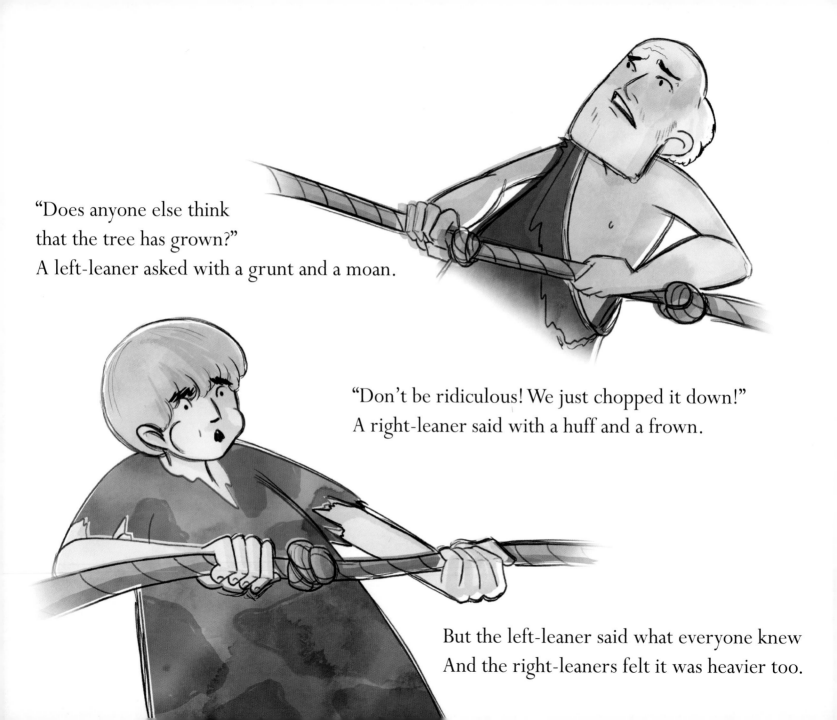

"Does anyone else think
that the tree has grown?"
A left-leaner asked with a grunt and a moan.

"Don't be ridiculous! We just chopped it down!"
A right-leaner said with a huff and a frown.

But the left-leaner said what everyone knew
And the right-leaners felt it was heavier too.

But the tree was no different,
Nor was the rope.
The hill had not changed,
Not even the slope.

Finally, each tribe looked to one another.
The left-leaners and right-leaners glared at each other.

"Aha! It's them," each tribe shouted and cried.
"It's because they are pulling too far to their side!"

So the left-leaners and right-leaners pulled harder and harder,
And away from each other they moved farther and farther.

"Can you believe those left-leaners? Where are they going?"
"Those reckless right-leaners don't know what they're doing!"

Doing their best, they pulled against one another
Until the tree stopped moving up the hill altogether.

Meanwhile, the valley continued to flood.
If they didn't act fast,
Home would be covered in mud!

Then something peculiar happened.
A right-leaner and left-leaner, who both were quite saddened,

Thought that maybe they should try talking instead.
"I'm going to the other side," they both said.

"Wait! Wait! Left-leaner, what are you doing?"
"If you leave now, right-leaner, we will all be ruined!"

Letting go of their ties,
toward the middle they walked.
But when they met in the middle,
they were totally shocked.

"Hello, left-leaner," said the right-leaner quite shyly.

"Hello, right-leaner," replied the left-leaner hesitantly.

"It seems we are stuck.
We are going nowhere."

"I noticed that too! It is too much to bear."

"What can we do to convince both our tribes
That they are pulling much too far to their sides?"

"I have an idea!"

They both said together,

"Let's trade places to help our tribes walk a bit straighter!"

But they worried as they looked at each other's tribes,
  And feared there was just too big a divide.

"I don't think your tribe will be happy to meet me."
  "Your tribe looks like they are really quite angry!"

"My tribe has good people. They are really quite kind."
   "My tribe is the same, they just have some pride."

                    "Neither tribe will admit they need any help."
                    "But maybe they would want to help someone else."

So our heroes went bravely to the opposite sides,
And to each tribe they called out without anger or pride.

"Hello, left-leaners! My right-leaning tribe could use some help."
"Right-leaners, we're in trouble, if I say so myself."

"Can you show me how to pull more to your side?"
The tribes both stopped with their mouths open wide.

"Of course we will show you how to pull to the left!"
"We would love to teach you to walk to the right!"

"Grab a spot right there and watch how we walk."
With the silence broken, they were happy to talk.

"You know, we would help any person we could.
We just thought you were pulling the tree into the flood!"

"Into the flood! Why would we do that?"
"We didn't know. We thought you'd gone mad!"

"From what we could see, you were going to fall.
We were pulling you away from that steep cliff wall!"

The right-leaners felt silly and a little ashamed.
Now they knew they'd pulled right, and were partly to blame.

And the left-leaning side felt quite silly too.
They saw they pulled further left than the others could do.

What happened next, you would never have guessed.
The two tribes walked straighter and made some progress!

But the top of the mountain was narrow and steep,
And the two tribes were forced to lessen their leans.

Unable to pull with their natural tilt,
They weren't quite as strong,
and they started to wilt.

"I'm not strong
when I cannot lean to the left."
"When I lean to the right
is when I'm at my best!"

"I know what to do," said the biggest right-leaner.
"We must use all our strengths, not what makes us weaker."

"I'll go to your side, and you come to mine,
And we'll balance each other to help with the climb."

So some left-leaners and right-leaners switched sides on each rope.
To be balanced and strong was their only hope.

Closer they climbed to the leak in the dam,
And they pushed the tree into place with a slam!

To this day, these tribes still lean one way or the other,
But they now see each other as sisters and brothers,

For they learned that when they all work together,
Whether they lean right or left doesn't really matter.

The End.